my big

sister

by Valorie Fisher

AN ANNE SCHWARTZ BOOK

Atheneum Books for Young Readers

New York   London   Toronto   Sydney   Singapore

ACKNOWLEDGMENTS

I am immensely grateful to Elinor Hills for her hard work, gracious smile, and delightful scowl. I would like to thank my son, Aidan, for being the perfect photographer's assistant and for lending me Bullet, Brooklyn's fastest goldfish; Bernadette Frishberg, a most expressive baby; Isadora and Miles Schappell-Spillman, whose Frances Popcorn was a lovely guinea pig of enormous talent; my mother, Susan Fisher, a rodent milliner extraordinaire; Mia and Romy Faucher-Mayhew for their much-too-much-loved dolls; and my brother, Kevin Fisher, for his insight into sisters, big and little. And I am deeply grateful for the continued support, enthusiasm, and friendship of Lee Wade and Anne Schwartz.

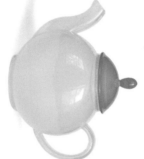

Atheneum Books for Young Readers
An imprint of Simon & Schuster Children's Publishing Division

1230 Avenue of the Americas

New York, New York 10020

Book design by Lee Wade

The text for this book is set in Filosophia.

Manufactured in China

First Edition

2 4 6 8 10 9 7 5 3 1

Library of Congress Cataloging-in-Publication Data

Fisher, Valorie.

My big sister / Valorie Fisher.

p. cm. "An Anne Schwartz Book."

Summary: Photographs and simple text illustrate
baby's view of what it is like to have a big sister.

ISBN 0-689-85479-X

[1. Sisters—Fiction. 2. Babies—Fiction.] I. Title.

PZ7.F5348 5 Mye 2004

[E]—dc21

2002006732

For Mom and Dad

This is my big sister.

It's hard for me to keep up with her.

She takes very
good care of me,

except when
she leaves me
with the neighbor.

She likes to pick out everyone's clothes.

My big sister kisses me,

and sometimes
she doesn't.

If I'm good,
she takes me
to the zoo